DUNCAN CULLMAN

PANDEMIC, POLITICS, THE RISE AND FALL OF HUMPTY DUMPTY

authorHOUSE®

AuthorHouse™
1663 Liberty Drive
Bloomington, IN 47403
www.authorhouse.com
Phone: 833-262-8899

Published by AuthorHouse 03/08/2021

ISBN: 978-1-6655-1927-4 (sc)
ISBN: 978-1-6655-1929-8 (hc)
ISBN: 978-1-6655-1928-1 (e)

Library of Congress Control Number: 2021904727

ESSENTIAL PEOPLE AND
ESSENTIAL REVOLUTION

If God has created us we are all essential our entire lives

We work to sustain ourselves and no matter what we do

It is essential that God must think it so thus no one is nonessential

As for non-essential business there are those who break our laws

Our laws and commandments were decreed for our own
protection

The transgressors once caught and sentenced go to our
essential prisons (to be essential prisoners)

Now Christ is coming to free us all from sin and death and
open the prisons

To redeclare that our work here on Earth had been essential
to His return

We are all His essential people especially when we pray to
be so

You regimes in power that consider us and our businesses
non-essential

You are playing God but you are not God you are blashemizing
your non-essential doctrines

Awaken all you essential lawyers stop cowering before the bench

You were born to defend the people and the laws and the
Constitution

Or if not then there will essentially be an essential revolution

THE METAPHYSICS OF OUR TIME

There are those who believe that when men stop sinning because all of them are reborn then karma will be extinguished in this world. Then time itself shall cease and all action. There will be no dharma other than to praise our Lord who shall then be visible. We shall rise like angels singing a heavenly chorus. This world will cease to exist because it cannot physically exist without sin.

Sin is the driving force in this world because it invites justice for a solution. Therefore this is a world of cops and robbers all of whom race about to delay justice and the end of time when justice shall complete itself

We are here to judge ourselves because we alone know what sins we may have committed. Will we be able to forgive ourselves knowing that God has already forgiven us?

There will be left on Earth no dharma duty to struggle against injustices when there is no longer any injustice. There will thus be no purpose left for us to continue to live here on this Earth. Our karma will have been released and forgiven and our dharma will be to serve God as Angel/s.

It will be as though Satan were removed completely as though cast into some invisible trench or pit. We shall be incorruptible.

When we finally understand time we shall be released from both time and sin as they are inseparable. Our own sins have created our own dharma and duty we need fulfill to erase our debt unless or until Christ shall intercede and forgive us our trespasses at which point we die instantaneously and arise as Angels.

NEAR TO ME

Sat, Jan 16, 2:14 AM)

Call on the Lord while He is near

When you are lost or before you become lost look for a beacon

Because the Lord alone is my light and salvation

On the open sea where waves crash against my boat in darkness

I do not know how near to me Leviathan that serpent lurks
beneath

If I do not pray then surely I am lost with no light to save me
no moon no stars

The sun itself may not rise on my tomorrow if I cannot pass
this night in prayer

What will become of me and who will there be who still remembers me

"O yes we knew him too bad he fell off his high castle wall thinking himself indestructible

Did he think he was Donald Trump or something like that?

Therefore call on the Lord well before you are a Humpty Dumpty

All the king's horses and all the king's men couldn't put Humpty back together

Again I pray save me my Lord from such catastrophe be my Savior

Die on a cross for me that I taste not death but rise with you

into your kingdom

To be in that room you have prepared for me where I will be

safe forever

For you have set a table before me in the presence of my enemies

You are near to me my breastplate of armour my shield and

buckler

I will not fear though I walk through the valley of death

because you are with me

Your anointed child who shall proclaim your greatness forever

who shall sing hymns

Let my song reverberate in the hills let my laughter continue
with friends

Let us sup together those of my own understanding who
earnestly pray

Bring us together as a nation of angels as a congregation of good

We are righteously calling your name in this darkness see us

Look down upon us have mercy that we may one day dwell
with you in Sion

MY FATHER'S HOUSE
(THE HOUSE OF ISRAEL)

Take sanctuary and rest in the House of the Lord of Israel

It is your father's house and was his father's and was Abraham's

It is a rock and a church this House of Israel to save you from
the storm

You cannot purchase it because God who dwells within and
without is also not for sale

Do not insult God and think He may be owned so do not
attempt to buy His house

There is of course the house of perdition, the synagogue of
Satan do not fall into that trap or snare

Live instead one hundred years in peace and understanding

The king is coming the king of Israel and the house belongs

not to him but to his heavenly Father

So dwell instead in a yurt or a tent or pay rent or be a house

sitter to be safe

It is the Lord Himself Who owns this house of sanctuary in

Zion

Go instead like Ruth and purchase a field to plant some seeds

that there will be a harvest by the righteous

Because not all who sow will reap and so not all who dwell in

houses will be happy

Only those who take refuge in the House of Israel shall escape

this current storm

This rafing fire and this raging virus, these tornados, hurricanes

and earthquakes will consume

Everyone who dwells in the houses of perdition shall become

lost in the sea of fire

Therefore take rest and sanctuary in your Father's house

because you are a child of the Lord who is his Lord

Try to understand this, fathom wisdom and be a sage very

learned

That you may live in peace forever with God

EMPTY YOUR MIND (THE MIDNIGHT HOUR)

Sleep and empty your mind awake refreshed. Awaken in the garden of Eden in innocence before you were born you were there with cherubs. This world is not your true home, Melchizedek, you are a priest sent here to glorify your Maker and Creator, the one God, Lord of hosts.

Sleep and dream because you are in the forest alone but safe away from the strife of everyday life in the populous world of hustle, the rat race of every city. Rest here in this sanctuary on a hill overlooking the valley, overlooking distant mountains. These hills are worn flat by time and glaciers. These hills are your home. These hills are where you were born in the arms of your mother. These hills extend even to peninsulas going into the sea.

Sleep well because you are of good conscience when you pray to your Lord it is like the finest verse ever written. It is like the Sermon on the Mount which was in fact a hill like this one.

God is here to dwell with you if you rest and wake refreshed then God will guide your pen to write pleasant verses. Write mostly about God because you cannot fully comprehend your

Lord. It would take over a trillion computers just to record what God has done in two dimensions but there are four.

Time has been created in order that there will be justice to show complete evidence of our God that he is good. At the end of time there will be no need for time itself when good shall destroy evil we shall all be risen and free of sin.

The time of Satan is nearing an end and this is an undeniable truth we see everyday we live. We see terrible things happen when we are in the wrong place there is war and destruction. Lord take me home away from this dangerous place. Take me up your hill that I may dwell with you in Sion.

Do not swear and do not covet what others have only leads them into sin. Monetary independence leads them away from God. That is why you have taken a mortgage and that is why you now work. You are no better than Job and if you pray to God then you will have all you need not what you want.

The Lord shall grant you refreshing dreams full of rest, puffy clouds and a view of sea and lakes. He will set you beside a gentle stream of righteousness, a brook of solitude where you may wash your clothes and face, where you may soak your hands and feet. God is good Therefore empty your mind. You are connected to your God, not independent from God because independence from God is death and destruction like Satan. So with pen in hand begin to write down these verses.

"In the beginning there was God."

God is the author of everything. He has given Lucifer the freedom to destroy himself. If you have children go to them. Go home to your wife while you still have one. The day of the Lord will be terrible none shall be left standing. At the end of time there will be only a theocracy for the angels...

IN SEARCH OF THE LOST CITY

In searching for the lost city that Citadel of our Lord in Zion

It is on the higher ground upon a hill not in a swamp

While I who am searching must confess I am lost

I am lost in this lower world now that I cannot see my Lord
and Creator

I am lost in the darkness of night as though in a dense fog

When will the gentle mountain breezes return and reveal to
me the sun and moon?

When will my star again shine and deliver the captives from
bondage?

Then the Red Sea shall part and the highway be made clear

for the escape of my people

We shall flee the oppressors and the Conquistadors and enter

Vilcabamba

Refuge shall not be denied to us we will enter Zealand hut in

the land of the living

Moses and Aaron shall ascend a high mountain and receive

the Commandments of our God

Elijah shall prophesy that Jesus and John will baptize with

water and fire

That the Holy Ghost will fill us with the love of our God

Wherein the land shall be made sweet with milk and honey

Beulah

The redeemed shall dwell there and be fallen no more from

the Garden

This is the second birth and the Resurrection it shall happen

within me that I be new

Because I shall love the Lord my God therefore I shall love

every man as my own brother and sister

So the Lost City I will enter and be lost no more for I am home

with my God

MAC STRODHAIL

In Maine on Rangeley Lake or is it Mooselukmeguntic there were wooden sidewalks between the cabins. The neighbors all called my grandfather "Mac" which means son. He didn't seem to love my father who had married his daughter, my mother Thais Heald MacBride.

There was an issue concerning my father who mostly wasn't there at all as his brothers in New York wouldn't give him the week off to vacation with his Gentile bride. I did my best waking up at six o'clock each morning and strolling those gangplanks before my mother even knew I was missing. The neighbors usually located me as I was just three and still cute.

My father divorced my mother after sending her to a mental institution one morning in an ambulance which came to pick her up screaming at them. They bodily dragged her out the front door against her will and drove off to my horror. My father soon appeared and announced,

'Now you'll do as I say! Go to your room!"

I wasn't very happy about his pronouncement nor his treatment of my mother so within ten years I packed my small bag and left home in full adolescence like the prodigal son I fled but unlike the prodigal son I had no money to spend on debauchery, just no money at all.

Perhaps I was bitter or very soon to be as things weren't going my way very smoothly at all. Being under twenty years old I was still cute somewhat and there are those amicable who help the young and lost. Mostly I was lost because I didn't know it was God who with everlasting kindness guides even the birds to find worms to eat. God was guiding me into a new wondrous adventure in faraway states where I met many new and kind people. After age thirty one doesn't meet these kinds of helpful souls. After age thirty one is everything but cute except for blond women with French Poodles. Those are the exceptions as perhaps maybe the little dogs need a bone?

So I, Mac Strodhail, wandered from adventure to adventure and met many fine young lassies who would sneak me home sometimes up a tree into a bedroom window from which I would exit 5AM.

God it seems was less and less pleased with my sordid

adventures though work and a few dollars were easy to find. I labored long with my young strong back not realizing it would not be so forever and thinking I might work easily all my life at these endless menial jobs.

Then there was Kate, a school teacher who took me in but labored each night with endless homework just like her students whose exams she corrected. So really she had a full life and no time for me except on weekends in mostly summer. Those were fun in lakes and ponds with canoes and sailboats. We loved campfires at the beach and throwing sticks for dogs. I suppose I had no real profession as I had left home before my father could train me in any skill. I could wipe my own ass. My mother had taught me that!

As a nine year old in Sunday School I had developed a strong crush on my thirteen year old teacher with blond hair and blue eyes. She taught me about Jesus that God loves us and Jesus was his only son.

"God made us all and he must love us too!" I protested only to learn that we are sinners but must be forgiven if we ask to be while forgiving those who trespass against us. I had run away from home a few years later and my father had interrupted my Christian schooling as he was Jewish and had adopted me so what was I then?

I would have an entire lifetime to discover exactly but without knowing my biological parents and their inherent dreams and skills I was mostly unguided and perpetually lost. I was bitter about this and took to alcoholic beverages. Then through this avenue to hell I wandered in search of whatever the devil would lead me to not just to observe it but to be envious of others in order to destroy them in some small way called deceit.

I had entered a new underworld of demons in Hades who began wrestling for my soul to aid and abet their attempt to destroy the Earth and everyone on the planet. The nightly news was always some ghastly affair in the bar where someone usually knew either a victim or a perpetrator of the crimes, perhaps a bar patron?

I wandered the entire lower forty eight states in this

fashion leaving behind a wanton trail of destruction, of broken hearts and promises. I even married for four months until Mrs. became pregnant. That was like hell and I pleaded for an abortion with no fine luck. It was not to be. She threw me out into the cold. I bought a bus ticket across the country. It was winter and the bus was warm and so was Florida where I arrived but it seemed no one wanted the likes of me. I was from the wrong side of the tracks and all could tell that. I swept and mopped the bar for free drinks all night long after closing then slept under a Palm tree until a coconut fell on my shoulder. I could have been killed. This was not my native state with far too many Latinos taking most of the good jobs. They were highly skilled and came from fathers who taught them well not like mine.

"Your heavenly Father loves you and sent his son to die in your place that you need not taste death itself" said the young evangelist standing over me where I was sleeping in my cardboard box on the sidewalk.

Now I was learning that I had another father, one who

actually cared for me and sent these young smartly dressed people to find and teach me daily. I was making some progress. I swept and mopped The Church of Christ every Sunday evening and had a free meal or two then three with the Pastor and his wife but I was not permitted to talk with their children or any children whatsoever. I didn't really like children except for young ladies which might come of age. it seems they were all worried about that at least concerning me. I was the bottom of the barrel and I would not be able to crawl out in their eyes even though I accepted Jesus as my Savior.

I didn't realize how the years were flying by and I became quite middle aged and gray when I received a letter in reply from my father who begged my forgiveness and pleaded with me to come home. It seems he had a change of heart and wished for my return and so I hopped on the bus much to the disappointment of my congregation who thought perhaps now they owned me like a slave.

My father now lives in a big mansion. I was thinking I had the wrong address when knocking on the door. A woman answered, a maid, who showed me to my room. It was very splendid. then came my father and his new charming wife. They were both full of tears as was I. My father was turning ninety years old and very gray but I still recognized him and he me.

Oh how good it is to come home and have family. I had been lost and wandering most of my life though the fault was not entirely my own. It is the nature of this world we live in full of confusion and many scattered lost sheep. Thanks to God who must love us dearly and wants to recollect us back into the sheepfold to be our loving Pastor Forever. Praise God who has given me my father back though perhaps only for a few short years full of remembrances and long stories into the evening hours though usually not past ten o'clock as he was now tiring more early.

I want you who are young to take heed and not leave home while still children like I did. I realize that many parents lack perfection. Tell them that they are loved by you as well as God, that God loves them and sent His only son to give his life upon the cross that they too might believe and be saved. that is all i wish for

THE WEDDING ON THE ROAD TO JERUSALEM

The wedding guest has arrived at my father's house and has been greeted by our indentured servant who coming out of the basement door exclaimed,

"Welcome to this royal wedding but first have yourself a strong drink because the bride upstairs is not yet ready and I fear she is in a bad mood because the groom is late. So others come into the basement with me or better yet we will go drink in your car in the driveway, Mr Bean."

So the two of them went off to find a bottle of whiskey.

Now the groom has come looking for the bride and he sees the two men drinking in the small white car so he inquires,

"Where is the wedding? Isn't this my father's house and why isn't the bride ready yet on this the longest of summer days, the June solstice because the son of man is going to appear in heaven at least in the mind of my beloved, the bride. She will soon be most glad and gay. The wedding guests will devour the wedding cake like ravenous wolves shortly thereafter like lions eating a straggling lame calf"

"Oh I see the bride is exceedingly ill with morning sickness and hasn't yet taken her medicine probably. Is she sleeping in the far room? I'll go throw stones at her window! Arise, arise my bride!" sings the groom to the upper window on the back side of the house while looking for some small people to throw at the window.

"Oh my groom is here!" exclaims the bride opening her eyes at the sound of breaking glass and a small stone landing on the floor beside her bed, then she adds,

"Where is my wedding guest, the best man?"

"My love my fair one where art thou, come away into the garden of your beloved!" cries the groom in a song of songs.

"Come away my beloved for we will soon be at my father's house together arm in arm and I will adorn your shoulders with a wreath of freshly picked flowers for the time is at hand!"

Meanwhile the servant and best man have fallen asleep as a morning fog now hides the small white car in the driveway from the view of even God in heaven.

The bride now rises up and looks for her medicine bag to consume her daily sum and quota of "Happy Pills" because the

Earth is now a sad planet due to global warming and a myriad of locusts eat everything in sight.

"My love, my love, have you yet seen our guest? Do please instruct him to enter my father's house through the front door lest he meet that awful servant of ours who will want a cigarette and a bottle of whiskey. I have prepared a room for him that where I slept as a child he might take a quick nap before the bachelor's party."

"Oh my beloved," cries the bride, "The servant is missing from the basement but I did see his wife and child drive off to Dunkin Donuts for their usual coffee and a doughnut for the child, I suppose!"

The best man and guest wakes up in the fog bank shivering and starts the small car's engine turning on the heater but the sleeping servant kicks the gear shift into reverse so the small car is now heading toward the small lake also shrouded in fog.

Do not tarry, do not be late for your wedding date when the son of man shall appear and the bride shall be most happy to see him. Because a thief has come to enter my father's house through the basement door now that the servant is missing having possibly gone gay so now the thief is ransacking the entire pile of clean laundry including the tuxedos and the wedding gown.

Many are called but few are chosen. Be sober and vigilant. Stand guard at the door and greet all the arriving guests because my father's house has many rooms. It is the size of an ark, it is like a ship, a vessel. The coming storms of winter will approach and the snowdrifts will pile high even up to the gables of the roof itself but you will be indoors and comfortable.

Take heed and come. The best man has been arrested for DUI and resisting arrest beside the lake. The servant has drowned because he could not swim. But his wife will open a thrift store from all the extra laundry of the hoarding newlyweds. The dogs have run off into the woods to chase porcupines. The wedding is for now on hold but predestined as perhaps are all due to the interference of angels. God bless them and God bless this house eternal.

THE REPUBLICAN PARTY OF
ABRAHAM LINCOLN

The Republican Party of father Abraham Lincoln which freed the slaves and reunited our nation

The Republican Party of father Abraham has been hijacked by a tyrant to divide our country

The Republican Party member of today who are advocating the overthrow of our democracy

Is there a tree high enough with sufficient branches from which they all might be hung

A tree of righteousness in service of our Lord, a tree of knowledge in our garden of America

The cherubs are its guardians and the angelic host including those who stand up against tyranny

Like Bernie Sanders and Mitt Romney but Susan Collins has
no courage

To call tyranny treason and this tyrant a Hitler sent from hell

Whose 140 followers are demonized under his spell of pure
madness

No one dares ride in his golf cart with him because he is mad
like Nebacaneezer

Soon he will be eating grass like the cows but wearing a senior
diaper

Because the party needs be purged of its Ted Cruz and Rudi
Gulianis who stand on the grassy knoll ready to shoot
Kennedy

There will be justice in the land of freedom a bell will ring from its high church tower

God and the people will restore order and decency and these crooks will go to the scaffolds

The tree of righteousness is waiting for them all and the trumpets are sounding

It is taps for America if she cannot take a bath in ocean waters a rogue wave will come

It will devour the Potomac it will devour the city of love it will smash Ellis Island and the Statue of Liberty

America as we know it shall be no more because traitors have risen to destroy her

GOD

Our God we have made a covenant with loves us conditionally. If we love our God then we are treated favorably, so we pray.

We pray that any references to God as a woman will be forgiven. She is most lovely under the apple tree, the daughter of Jerusalem and her banquet is love.

God himself is not exactly love but requires obedience? Jesus loved us all unconditionally like a father not conditionally like a mother who may have spanked us.

So New Jerusalem is where we will live and she is a diadem like a diamond in the sky. She is lovely as the angels are who protect her. Jerusalem on the Earth is the geometrical center of the land masses or nearly so. She is hidden by a cloud of moisture wherein her flock of sheep and the children live protected by God. They also must choose to protect themselves however God instructs them.

An atheist is still loved by God as are the heathen who wander like vagabonds who flee lands of lawlessness knowing that somewhere there is justice in the land of the living.

If I lie to you then this is terrible karma and my future is surely in doubt because the dishonest will not see God. They are liars and sorcerers, everything vile and offensive.

Know the truth and preach the Gospel of Jesus Christ because he is faultless and pure. He never lies to us even though his parables sometimes bewilder us.

If God loves us conditionally because of our covenant then some people might be confused and think God is our mother. There is some confusion because Baal the fertility god of the heathen was like a golden cow.

Surely most of us in this modern educated world of I-phones are not like the Incas in Vilcabamba worshipping a large rock from the Ice Age deposited at the edge of the Amazon.

Hyana-Capac, the last Inca, said before his execution in Cuzco, Peru

"Look my people how I am being executed by these invaders with their own God whose son is Jesus Christ"

God please forgive me if I have erred or told any falsehoods and or lies. Miryam from Argentina wrote me to tell me that the Hebrew God is never a woman. Therefore I must clarify myself in the eyes of God.

There are some other thoughts I have been given but tonight I am not to write them down so these clarifications are back in their cloud which is the mind of our Father from whom all our truths originate. Amen

2000 YEARS AGO VERSUS TODAY

Over two thousand years ago a doctor named Jesus said that what can harm a man most is what comes out of his mouth even more than what goes into his mouth.

Now that we are all wearing cloth face coverings let us remember what our healer and doctor Jesus said because apparently he spoke the truth to some very high degree of proficiency. He was very knowledgeable more so than even our own president apparently.

Perdition and loss occurs to us when we speak falsehoods and make up lies about our neighbors even though it seems funny to us on the schoolbus when young to say that some other child's mother is a monster and/or that their house is full of field mice, toads and boa constrictors or perhaps they all practice witchcraft.

I am not Dr. Fauci nor a White House advisor on national health nor our president's personal physician and most of us don't want any of these difficult jobs such as president or first lady.

Apparently people though espousing to be "Christians" don't really adhere to very much of what Jesus the Christ actually said or did. We are witnessing an entire cult of self-proclaimed "Ministers of the Spirit" who have brought us to the brink of perdition and hell or else why are we experiencing these plagues reminiscent of "End Times of Our World".

"Go in peace, my brothers and profess the truth is what I have told you."

Therefore it is apparent that Jesus was our very best of friends and could be trusted as such even more than the majority of our so-called friends who lead us to the edges of cliffs and laughingly tell us,

"You can fly like Superman!"

Our president was wearing this outfit as a mild joke but maybe he was dead serious.

This brings us back to 2000 years ago when men were more advanced than we are today evidently. We have been backsliding into an abyss...

The blind shall see, the deaf shall hear and the lame shall walk in the Kingdom of Heaven in the presence of our Lord and Savior.

"I am the Way and the Truth and the Life, Nobody comes to the Father but through Me!"

"I am the Door, knock and it shall be opened"

THE BUM IN THE BIG WHITE HOUSE

How did that bum get in there to begin with?

Maybe the American people felt sorry for him> Get over it!

Felt sorry his father only gave him a graduation present of
    $431 million

He didn't even graduate? Well there are stupid children

Now we have one in the big White House who won't leave

He has nowhere to go, he has nowhere to go and hide

Creditors are coming after him in droves

Then there is the war crimes tribunal he waged a war on the poor

Somebody give him a KITA! You're fired!

Go down to the Bowery and bring your bottle in a paper bag

If you love only yourself you are a has-been

Goodnight and goodbye and stop crying in your beer, Heinrich!

VERMONT AND NEW HAMPSHIRE MARRIAGE PROPOSAL

Rather than being divided and split apart the two states of Vermont and New Hampshire should buck the CDC guidelines and enter into matrimony. We have a common river, the Connecticut and so our cultures are intertwined as are our two economies. Vermonters need an extra place to work and shop and New Hampshire has skiers that can add tourist dollars to Vermont ski areas.

The problem remains fine dining. People want to talk in restaurants and without masks on. Let us remind them they are there to eat and when not eating but gabbing put their masks back on please.

Dividing the states the CDC under this president is further dividing the country into fifty nations plus Puerto Rico independence.

It is not so impossible to track people let us not further damage our economy with this political bickering.

Will you marry me?Yes

Massachusetts married Maine and Rhode Island to Connecticut.

The land is now Beulah like in the Bible

God is Alive!

Duncan Cullman

3:03 AM

Write all these things down when the people are ready to receive new knowledge. Write down that once forgiven they will not suffer the past because now is their new day of liberation and love. They will be free.

Love is coming to save them because the Master is perfection and living in divine perfection. In the fullness of love there is no past and karma(debt) is released. So are the children of Israel released from bondage and slavery in Egypt and given the promised land which is this brand new day of now. As for tomorrow do not worry about it because with the past now forgiven the dharma duty of tomorrow is light. The burden and yoke of past sin is released and the beast is no longer like the oxen needing to be whipped. These new oxen gladly work because they are loved so they know all duty is just to love and be loved.

As for tomorrow, have faith that Our Father shall take care of us like the birds, do they reap and sow?

Write this all down because the people are ready to be united in love in a united state of love. Young people suffer because they are overwhelmed by their senses of touch, smell and taste.

There is an evildoer in this world whose past is notorious and for this reason he does have the very most dismal future possible. He will be put in chains and thrown into a pit for over one thousand years in a lake of fire where there is no water to drink and his own throat will grow parch like a man lost on a hot day in the Sahara.

Now you my children will not go with him nor be lost because love has found you. You are now so loved by God your creator who speaks into your hearts with the utmost pleasure which is love itself.

Those who love will establish the kingdom of God which is what every family desires, a perfect home, where all within are loved and cared for and each cares for the other. They dwell like sheep in a flock because the Great Shepherd is there with them standing guard. If one gets lost the shepherd retrieves it and brings it back into the herd.

This world will not endure forever but the kingdom of God is eternal and shall always. There has been just too much sin here on Earth and its secure present is unsustainable. It's very karma of debt to sin is gloom and doom. When you watch the nightly news you realize that evil has had its own day but those who follow wickedness are being chased by the police. It shall always be that way. The devil is on the run being pursued and will find no sanctuary.

In the meanwhile you shall be saved because the Master Himself talks to you and tells you this is how it will be as you grow older and wiser. God himself will try to find a way into your heart if you are willing to listen and be loved. Then you shall hear the Word of God which is Love and you will love others as you wish to be loved yourself because God loved you when He She created you.

I am sorry we must all die one day for our sins because of our ignorant ways this is our dharma duty to return to God and dwell there with God in His Holy City New Jerusalem. On planet Earth the old Jerusalem is still at war and being besieged by the nonbelievers.

They were unable to kill the Master because He did not sin and thus returned where his disciples beheld his full Glory. We shall all soon reign with Him in Paradise and in the meanwhile we invite His Kingdom to be here on Earth in our very presence. We go to church and pray if we are too weak to do that at home or under a tree in our garden.

So pray to your living God because there is no other. Balzebub has no future and his followers end up in despair, panic and bad conscience like psychopaths. Do not follow him like a sociopath. There is no future in lawlessness but prison where all are tortured at least mentally if not physically abused as well.

Come to New Jerusalem I beseech you in the name of my Father. There is no other place of refuge but with God himself herself. She he is waiting with open arms for your return, now come my child and be with the Master your Pastor and take your place in peace and salvation

IN SION OUR DAYS AND
NIGHTS NEVER ALONE

Our God is both with us and within us

Who is our salvation who restores us who gives us life

Who breathes our every breath who sees our every sight

He is not far distant on some other isolated planet He is on
every planet

He is on every continent and with every person who calls to
Him for help

If our president is godly then he is for us not against us he is a
man of the people

Not above everyone not a superman but a common humble man

There are those who love arrogance because they are both
ignorant and arrogant

Let them stumble and fall into the lion's pit let them dwell
with serpents

Our God Who is with us His anointed will allow them their
destruction

They bring it upon themselves who are without God and He
is without them

God has gone on an extended vacation away from them who
have no Holy Days no holidays

You imagine that God is in some distant place and He is
distant from you

Come back to me my God that we may dwell together in Sion

Make Your sun rise and shine upon our day spent together

and give us an evening together too with stars and moon

Suree Suri has stolen the election (Walking Encyclopedias

Have Defeated Our Don)

MY FELLOW REPUBLICANS

There is a virus for one;and for two there is global warming. Drinking "Billy Beer" will not make these things go away. Living in denial of them has lost us this 2020 Pandemic Election.

There is one other key ingredient which relates to compulsive psychopathic lying. Should we follow a criminal cyber bully big shot just because he has a limousine plus a yacht plus a big jet and is a television celebrity we will do harm to the country even when our portfolios are enriched greatly.

So let us be smart rats all and jump off this sinking ship of this antichrist and false messiah who has no future. The devil with those who have misled us with cronyism from their bully pulpits of hypocrisy. Our true father is "Father Abraham" Lincoln for whom this Lincoln Memorial was built.

Donald Trump can be best remembered for the good things he did even though he seemed to have gotten lost in some dense fog or was it smoke from smoldering Democratic Institutions like Obamacare?

The American people regardless of ethnicity or gender

identity now all have I-phones which they can use to boost their intelligence with simple questions like,

"Suree, who should I vote for in this election?"

So we must regard them as well informed even if they might have flunked life in general as at least they have these phones with 32 MG. These new phones can pass most written exams in a vast majority of universities.

Suree it seems has a doctorate in everything under the sun. Thus every Dick, Jane and Harry with an I-phone is now a walking encyclopedia. Very hard it is to lie to these people when you can hear in the backdrop someone named Suree has the answer and blurbs it out,

"Porkchops Pompeo and Pence are lying!"

"Donald assumes Melania won't divorce him in the next 24 hours but then when they are over, wait..."

"So please consider my candidacy, my name is Suree and my game is still the same..."

THE GREAT VICTORY SPEECH
(THINE KINGDOM COME ON
EARTH AS WELL. . .)

My fellow Americans and also those who might want to visit our shores including those who never will to whom we send our warm embrace.

You might have heard by now that I lost my son and my first wife. What this means is I may be a lonely father without a family to receive my love so now you will be my family. I extend my love and gratitude to you all.

Now I have all this extra love to share (A father can save many children.). So now that I have won your votes I can be like a father to you if you chose to add me to your extended family. Add me to your living room on TV. Add me to your kitchen and boil some water for us so that we might have soup together where I may reside in your home at least spiritually if you so chose.

I want you to call me "Daddy". My house is a great white house but it is your house too. It is the house of all the American people who are winning this great victory we call love. Though there may not be room enough to fit all of you at once, feel welcome and think of this "White House" as your own. It belongs to the American people, not to some king. but to everyone who lost a grandfather because now I will be your grandfather.

And so my dear children all across America if America is to lead the world then I am speaking to everyone in every nation as well. It matters what a president says, yes it does.

Think of me as your great grandfather, a super Daddy who loves you all. I loved my own son so now I love you with that same love. I love you all because the health of this family, this family we call the world, the health of every family in this world is interconnected. If a plague or pandemic breaks out it affects us all. That is why we are endorsing a universal health care system to eradicate disease worldwide to prevent disease worldwide. Once these pandemics break out they are not so easy to contain and cost our economies dearly. They rob us of our extra vacation money but much worse of course they rob us of our loved ones.

They rob us of healthy workers in the fields to pick our vegetables and fruit. They rob the food right off our own tables to feed us. Once these pandemics attack they attack all of us.

So therefore my children,

Therefore you are my children everywhere. I have dedicated this speech to call you home. I am calling you to join me in one big extended family, the family of man where we will all be together. We are all on the same team now. There is no more "My team wins and your team loses".

We are on the same playing field: all of us are the winners here together who play the game. But "Family" is no game. Family is all of us together. That's whose president I must be to unite this nation, a president of each and every one of you worldwide who calls upon me.

If you can trust me then I can be your president.

This is both the victory and concession speech: that I love you all equally, of every race, creed color gender, of every political leaning. I will try my very best to be a good father to you all. This is how a president must serve his people. He serves the goodness of his own heart with compassion born from God to be shared among men as equals

God is looking down from heaven ordaining a brand new day for our United States

LAND OF THE RICH WHO FREELY SPEND

While in urgent care at my local hospital today I was informed by my attractive physician not to worry about the COVID vaccine as it would not be available for the general public. I thought as a senior citizen that I may be first in line but without underlying health issues I am grouped at age 73 into the general public which are no better than test animals for further testing. Pharmacists who are regarded as essential workers as well as doctors and lawyers, judges and politicians will be in line for the vaccine first now that America has become a privileged state primarily for those with privilege and much lesser so for those of us earning less money as it seems we are second class citizens and expendable.

This brings us directly into a constitutional crisis wherein all men were created equal but are now separated by rank and file into essential and nonessential. Basketball and other professional athletes must be essential whereas amateur sportsmen like duck hunters and fishermen are nonessential unless on television.

Hollywood actors and actresses must be essential as they

are on high salary like directors and mayors. We may therefore assume that it is more who you know than what you know in America as the COVID vaccine will be political.

The pandemic has come to challenge all of our wits and allegiances.

Our dutiful privileged president states that he has won re-election and doesn't want to wait four more years to be re-elected. Everything here in America is moving at lightning speed away from our old values of justice into this new justice for everyone that can buy it.

I am sure there will be some exceptions for anyone willing to pay top dollar to receive the COVID vaccine. Since when has money not been a pivotal force in America land of the free but even more so land of the rich who freely spend and support Twitler...

CONCESSION SPEECH

My fellow Americans,

Most of you did not even know I was running for president as my name did not appear on the ballot where you voted and even in grade school I had some difficulty spelling it correctly so you most likely would have also had you attempted to write me in.

One of my big problems was that I did not even vote for myself in this election though in years past I might have once.

It is difficult to lose especially considering that the other presidential candidates were of no special substance being both senile and argumentative with zero grace.

There is evidently not even one fit American for this highest office as we are all equally brainwashed by American television which contains commercial advertising telling us we must indeed buy everything in life including your vote. That Donald understood this particularly well when he tossed his MAKE AMERICA GREAT AGAIN hat into your willing hands and you were fool enough to wear it.

Now we have a nation of idiots like you who are wearing these baseball hats singing in unison,

"Take me out to the ballgame, take me out to the show!"

You think you are worthy to stand at the plate and swing a bat? The manager in the dugout is God. He will determine where you are in the lineup. You better behave well on the bench so you will even be included in the game.

If nominated I will not accept. If elected I will not serve. I am just a total loser which brings me to your vote of confidence in me and you never did cast it. Therefore I declare myself an American Indian very likely to return to my reservation you have prepared for me in the Mojave Desert. I best fill my canteen.

So I am on my way into the Mojave and Death Valley on that long road to nowhere totally unemployed as I lost my one chance for my very first job in life to be your personal President of these United States. Judging by the election results I would hardly think so.

You can join me there in Mojave please bring some blankets

as I forgot mine and the nights are cold even lonely. Maybe we can find some stray dogs for friends if you bring a can of dog food. Once you feed them they never forget for a lifetime. Humans are not like that at all you may have taken notice that your best friends of long ago are nowhere to be seen. Exactly. Now we have the root of this problem; it is our human nature. No human is fit to govern over any other whatsoever. Only God has the right to judge us and decree our futures. You think you can do it by buying stock in my company you think you can own me like a slave? I thought we abolished that. Evidently not.

I concede that we were both slaves of that same system by watching American television. I was in Austria once where the TV was owned by the state and was just one channel so as not to confuse everyone like here in America where we watch "The Bachelorette". This is confusing as a grown woman has to kiss every potential boyfriend like some flippant teenager. no wonder she gets totally upset and cries. Each one wants to enslave her.

No one has given you the right to enslave another. Turn off that television please HD or 3D or whatever. Do not vote for me simply because I do not want the job of entertaining you daily on television which is now the job description of American President. We will be better off as a couple of unemployed in the Mojave because during the day there it is much too hot to work. At night our hands and feet might freeze. We might construct an adobe but without water we will not be there long enough.

I want to take this last opportunity to thank you for not voting for me as you would have expected something from me like an economy or a job to hire you. You are just standing there and not being creative inventing something. Why in the hell do you think I would want you on my team anyway? I'll pitch and you swing the bat if you can do anything at all, play ball

HOLDING OUT HIS CONCESSION FOR A FULL PARDON (THE REAL NOT FAKE NEWS)

Apparently the Don is holding out for a full pardon from President Elect Joe Biden before he concedes this election. It's not working so well evidently as slow Joe doesn't like being called slow and he wants his own son pardoned by the Trump Administration for some misdemeanors.

Donald himself has likely committed worse than misdemeanors rumored as tax fraud plus cyber bullying plus obstruction of justice and whatever happened to that guy he murdered on Madison Avenue or was it an underage female?

It looks like the negotiations were going less than well with all these nefarious recounts of votes in Upper Michigan, Lake Superior and Three Points of Des Troit (Detroit). Donald is looking for forty plus extra electoral votes somewhere maybe in the thin blue air.

Okay so maybe we should forgive each other and Donald too? However he is such a compulsive liar and crook trying to make Al Cappone great again! There must be some deep feces behind the scene somewhere and we are not beholding it, the reporters have not dug deep enough into Russian Scorched

Earth Policies as Donald's Legionaries were raiding the Baltic Coast perhaps like the horny Vikings they are.

Come on, Joe, you can pardon him if you have something in writing like a plea deal but really it must be up to the Supreme Court to find that the President is out of his tree completely.

So Donald will do time in the "White Collar " Looney Bin instead complete with Tennis Courts and an eighteen hole golf course and wife visitation rights plus children. Mar Lago will be converted into a Federal Sanatorium for Trump Supporters like Kelianne McEnany and Mike Pence

THE PARABLES

The parables have come to us from God through a man, Jesus who proclaimed himself to be the original son of his father God. So be it that other men have written parables but they are not the true authors as God is the author of this entire world and man is merely a medium through which God might proclaim himself. Therefore man who enables these stories sent from God to be manifest makes God manifest among us all that we might listen and have sweet music fill our ears.

The Word of God is the music of every universe because our God is universal and is the power of love that gives us life and breath.

Once upon a time there was a man who bought some property hoping that he would be happy with a home there. Yet he was very lonely living there in the deep woods. So he chopped down some trees and made a cabin with the trees and planted some grass and bought some farm animals so he would not be lonely anymore.

Then he had a brilliant idea as it began to snow. He would invite over his neighbors for a snowshoe race up and down his hill on the side of the small mountain. Winter can be long and boring if one does nothing at all. So go sir crazy and make skis or snowboards or skates in the work shed.

Then a rogue appeared at the bottom of his hill and proclaimed himself to be the fastest of very fast skiers and challenged everyone in town to a snowshoe and ski race.

So the participants agreed to a championship vertical challenge ski race with a cookout afterward and they brought delicious things to eat and drink. It turned out that the rogue was indeed fast but our man on the hillside was even faster. The rogue not to be outdone challenged our man to a skating race across the pond and the rogue finally triumphed.

Is there a moral to this story? Well the time went by and no one was bored as they had many stories to write down about all the other people they met.

Jesus did not have a home but wandered throughout the kingdom with endless stories about everything and everyone and God his father in heaven.

Hearing this our man shook his head because he was afraid

to leave his own property for more than a few hours. He usually went straight home after going into town for supplies

So who was happier our man or Jesus who wandered everywhere and met everyone then alive? Our man wanted to meet everyone but lacked faith in their good intentions. He thought if he left his home for too long a period of time he might get arrested or crucified or killed by highwaymen.

So our man stayed home and fretted and pondered because the world was a worrisome place. The rogue had he not won the skating race would have wanted a bobsled race or a biathlon race. It worried the man and he stayed up late into the night watching television. Yet television worried him even more as it was mostly bad news'

So he began reading books and among his favorite was the Bible. It is the book of life and in it he found himself to be alive and living. Every word he spoke came from somewhere, hell or heaven, angels or demons. He began to sort out different expressions until he found love.

A woman appeared and in her hair was a rainbow and in

her eyes were stars. Her smile contained both the sun and moon. Now he was complete and she bore a child, Immanuel.

"He will save us all for when we grow old he will bring water from the distant river and tell us stories to make us happy that he too has met God our creator who lives not very far away at all."

WAAAGH

WAAAGH I am the president you voted me in because Daddy

    left me 431 million

Because I funded construction for fifty TRUMP TOWERS

    Waah

I am being cheated in this rigged election by DEMO

CRATS

Backed by big interests and big corporations even my son says

We must GO TO WAR over these election results STAND

    BY KKK

WAAAGH

I've always had my way because Daddy and Geoffrey Epstein

    let me WAAH

I will be filing lawsuits to block any more voting which if

    against me MUST BE ILLEGAL

WAAAGH I hate to lose in fact for me losing is just not

    possible because I AM YOUR KING Waaah

The media has been very unfair in their socialist communist

    agenda for Marx and Bernie WAAGH

This election is being stolen by liberals and homosexuals with

ties to CHINA

Where the virus was invented solely to defeat me and make

AMERICA self-destruct into left wing Black Fatchism

Therefore I am calling out THE PROUD BOYS and THE

KKK to fight in the streets

Until my eternal presidency is restored

I ALONE HAVE MADE AMERICA GREAT BECAUSE

I AM GREAT Don't you dare forget it WAAAGH

"Donald, I want a divorce" Who said that? Waah

WAAAGH!

WAAAGHA

GO AND SIN NO MORE

Dear Reader,

Behold in Zion is born to you a Savior who will deliver you
from sin and bondage

Come and be my anointed says the Lord your God without sin
you are immortal

Go and sin no more and escape the second death much worse
than the first

Without sin there is no karma no debt to pay and nothing
harmful coming your way

Therefore you will abstain from self-destruction, drugs and
alcohol

Because you no longer need such things now you will be free

To join the great liberation of my people every one of whom is
    inscribed in my sacred heart

So go and sin no more and preach this good news that we love
    one another as God loves us first

Therefore are we like batteries of the holy spirit which has
    entered us and charged us

I charge you also my each and every friend I show you
    compassion and respect

You are each and every one born of God to be holy and dwell
    with me in Sion

You must love yourself as you love others we are all connected
together

Without time there is only Me your God I dwell in each and
every one of you like a spark

I caused you to be born to discover love that is who we are for
without love you will perish

Do not die do not wither away but come to me my people for
we are one

We are of one loving God not many and we will sit on the
mount with Jesus

With Moses and Elijah and Mohammed and everyone who
prophesies truth

I realize this is a hard lesson to learn online in a pandemic so

I will end it

In order that we attend a large service to be held for all my

people in person togetherr

In Sion

SAILING WITH HANS

To Hans and Susan

For some lucky reason we decided not to sail across Lake
   Champlain

Maybe it was all those white caps waves splashing

Maybe it was because there were no other sailboats in the lake
   with sails still flying

Two of them had pulled down their sails to troll with their
   motors

Hans's Lightning was too small for a motor and the jib was
   working just fine racing along the shore well still a few
   hundred yards out with Burlington still miles away

Maybe it was Susan screaming in my ear that he's trying to kill us I doubted that

Maybe it was the bow underwater like a German U-boat in the Atlantic

Finally at reappeared after a few nervous seconds waves pouring over us

Help bail some water Hans passed us a small bucket

Halfway across the lake or more the birds on Bird Island had cried some insults at us proclaiming their niche

I screeched back at them all I don't want your eggs just teach me to fly

Soon we were almost home to shore we pulled down the sails

as the wind still pushed us in its gail force

"Maybe we can sail next week?" cried Hans like one of those

birds I laughed in relief as it was almost over

Susan looked at me doubtfully but then she smiled when her

feet landed on the dock

Just another day on the lake beamed our Captain Hans

We haven't seen him in months as he's racing his dirt bike over

the jumps at age 67 pushing it a little as I would say

It now is beginning to snow and ski areas will open with Hans

carving race turns like a madman

Well I suppose I am one of those too and Susan besides me

on her snowboard

She had even been a figure skater in her youth competing

in Stockholm when terrorists bombed the train station

beneath her window

I had my own thrilling moment racing my skis over Tuckerman's

Headwall

We were all much younger then but still our hearts remain so

We fly like birds on that island in Lake Champlain screeching

our narrow niche in this world

We drove away as the red sun set upon our long day

(Each and every one of us has an incredible story as we are all

God's children)

Printed in the United States
by Baker & Taylor Publisher Services